This book belongs to

_____

Published by Advance Publishers

© 1998 Disney Enterprises, Inc.
All rights reserved. Printed in the United States.
No part of this book may be reproduced or copied in any form
without the written permission of the copyright owner.

Written by Ronald Kidd
Illustrated by Yakovetic, David Scott Smith, and Jody Daily
Produced by Bumpy Slide Books

Story based on the Walt Disney motion picture, DUMBO,
suggested by the story, Dumbo, the flying elephant, by Helen Aberson and Harold Perl.
Copyright 1939 by Rollabook Publishers, Inc.

ISBN: 1-57973-005-1

10 9 8 7 6 5 4 3 2

Dumbo, the little elephant with the big ears, was the star of the circus. Every time he arrived in a new town, people would crowd into the big top to see his amazing show. They were never disappointed.

With Timothy the mouse perched in his hat,

Dumbo would climb to the top of the tent and jump off. Just as he was about to hit the ground, he would flap his ears and take off flying through the air! The crowds would cheer as he rocketed by, grinning and waving his trunk.

Dumbo loved his new life. He loved the cheers and excitement. Most of all, he loved the speed. The other elephants plodded; Dumbo zoomed. The other elephants slept late. Dumbo got up with the sun. The other elephants chewed slowly and deliberately. Dumbo gulped down his food so he could fly off in search of more adventures.

Dumbo grew impatient with anything that took a long time, especially chores. He would zip around the circus, tackling one duty after another but never spending much time on anything. As a result, he didn't always do a good job.

"Slow down, Dumbo," his mother would call to him. "Remember, anything worth doing is worth doing well."

But Dumbo did not listen. He was much too busy speeding around.

Even Casey Junior was too slow for Dumbo. He and Timothy would ride on the train for a while, but then Dumbo would grow impatient.

Before Timothy knew what was happening, the two of them would be high above the train, flying ahead to the next town.

"It's a great view from up here," said Timothy. "Too bad it's going by so fast!"

On one trip, after an especially hard day of
travel, the train pulled into town late in the afternoon.
Dumbo and Timothy, who had arrived hours ago,
settled in to watch as the elephants started putting
up the circus tent.

The elephants began work in their slow, careful way. First they unloaded the tent and tent poles. Then they waited for the roustabouts to dig the holes for the poles, making sure they were just the right size.

Dumbo fidgeted as he watched. Timothy said, "Too slow for you, kid? Sorry, but that's just the way it is with elephants — well, most elephants."

The elephants were just about to raise the tent poles when the ringmaster said, "It's getting dark, everybody. Let's call it a day. We'll finish setting up tomorrow."

As the elephants plodded back to the train, Dumbo flew over to join them. He found his mother and trotted along beside her feet.

"Come along, sweetheart," she said, smiling. "Time for bed."

Dumbo snuggled up to his mother and tried to sleep, but he couldn't. He decided to take a little walk instead. Soon he found himself out by the circus tent that was lying on the ground.

"I can put this up in no time," thought Dumbo. And he set to work.

Timothy, meanwhile, was having a dream. He was on a boat in the middle of a storm, riding the waves up and down. He looked off into the distance and saw a giant wave moving toward him.

"Hold on tight!" he called. "Here comes a big one!"
The wave hit, and Timothy was thrown into the air.
Grabbing the side of the boat, he hung on for dear life.

Just then Timothy woke up. He found that he was indeed hanging on, but not to a boat. He was dangling from Dumbo's hat as the little elephant flew back and forth in the moonlight.

"Dumbo, what are you doing?" cried Timothy.
"It's the middle of the night!"

Scrambling back into the hat, Timothy peered over the side. That's when he saw what was happening. Dumbo was putting up the circus tent!

Unlike the other elephants, though, Dumbo
wasn't working slowly. He was moving as fast as
he could. And for Dumbo the flying elephant, that
was very fast indeed.

"Uh, listen, kid," said Timothy, "this is a pretty big job."

Dumbo kept working.

"You know," said Timothy, "it may be harder than it looks."

Dumbo kept working.

"Even if you can do it," said Timothy, "the other elephants won't be happy."

Still Dumbo kept working.

Dumbo had thought he could finish in a few hours. But he found that the job would take a lot longer than that, even for a speedy elephant.

He dragged the heavy poles into the holes in the ground. Then he tried to tie ropes to the poles to hold them steady — but the ropes were hard to tie, so he tossed them aside.

Finally Dumbo brought out the big canvas tent and pulled it over the tent poles.

"I don't know," said Timothy, eyeing his friend's work. "That tent looks a little shaky to me."

But Dumbo thought the tent looked fine. And he knew the others would be impressed when they found out how quickly he had put it up.

Late that night a cold wind began to blow. It ruffled the grass and made the leaves shiver. Gathering strength, it bent the trees over and pushed the storm clouds across the sky. By the time it reached the circus, the wind was howling.

As Dumbo slept, the tent flapped and shook. Without ropes to hold them down, the posts gave way one by one. Finally, in a tremendous gust of wind, the big top came crashing to the ground.

Dumbo was up early the next morning to admire his work. When he peered outside, he was shocked. Tent poles were scattered like twigs, with the tent twisted around them.

Timothy gulped. "Uh-oh, kid," he said. "I think we've got a problem."

Dumbo and Timothy weren't the only ones watching. So were all the other performers, including the elephants. They had been planning to finish putting up the tent that morning. Now everyone wondered whether the circus would open that day at all.

Timothy stammered, "Dumbo was just trying to help — honest." Oops! Now everyone knew who had caused the mess.

Mrs. Jumbo stood beside her son. "All of us want the circus to open on time," she said. "If we work together, maybe it still can."

"You think Dumbo could help?" asked Timothy. She replied, "I suppose so — if he promises not to rush."

And so the elephants began, with Dumbo working alongside them. They gathered up the tent poles. They untangled the tent. Then the roustabouts dug new holes and the elephants raised the poles once again.

Dumbo was amazed to see that even though the elephants moved slowly, the job went quickly, because everyone worked together.

Dumbo and his friends were still trying to finish when people began to arrive to buy tickets. With the crowd watching in fascination, the elephants hoisted the big top into place. Then Dumbo flew high into the air and placed a banner at the very top.

"We did it!" cried Timothy. "The circus is going to open on time!"

That day Dumbo gave his best performance ever. Stepping off a high platform, he fell toward the ground. Then, at the last minute, he started to fly.

He raced around the big top as fast as he could. Then, remembering what he had learned, Dumbo slowed down.

Now he noticed that the crowd was no longer a blur. He could see every face, and each one was smiling.

Dumbo slowed down even more. He wanted this happy feeling to last a long, long time.

*F*ast, faster, fastest!
Speed is lots of fun.
But fastest isn't always best
When work is to be done.
Slow, slower, slowest!
If you try it, you can tell
That anything worth doing
Is a thing worth doing well!